W9-AWS-491

# Noggin and Bobbin
## In the Garden

Written and Illustrated by Olivier Dunrea

GoodYearBooks

Noggin and Bobbin
in the garden.

2

Pulling weeds.

Noggin and Bobbin
in the garden.

6

Singing! Whistling! Working!

Digging potatoes.

Picking tomatoes.

Picking cherries.

Packing berries.

Noggin and Bobbin
in the garden.

Singing! Whistling! Working!

Off to their picnic they go.
Singing! Whistling! Laughing!
Mmmm.